Dear Parents and Teachers,

Reading chapter books is a very exciting step in your child's life as a reader.

With Hello Reader Chapter Books, our goal is to bring the excitement of chapter books together with appropriate content and vocabulary so that children take pride in their success as readers.

Children like to read independently, but you can share this experience with them to make it even more rewarding. Here are some tips to try:

- Read the book aloud for the first time.
- Point out the chapter headings.
- Look at the illustrations. Can your child find words in the text that match the pictures?
- After you or your child finishes reading a chapter, ask what might happen in the next chapter.
- Praise your child throughout the reading of the book.
- And if your child wants to read alone, then take out your own book or magazine and read sitting side by side!

Remember, reading is a joy to share. So, have fun experiencing your child's new ability to read chapter books!

Francie Alexander
Vice President and Chief Academic Officer
Scholastic Education

ISBN 0-439-57348-3

Text copyright © 2003 by Brian James.
Illustrations copyright © 2003 by Bryan Langdo.
All rights reserved. Published by Scholastic Inc.
SCHOLASTIC, HELLO READER, and associated logos are trademarks and/or registered trademarks of Scholastic Inc.

12 11 10 9 8 7 6 5 4 3 2 1   3 4 5 6 7 8/0

Printed in the U.S.A.
First printing, October 2003

SPOOKY HAYRIDE

by Brian James
Illustrated by Bryan Langdo

SCHOLASTIC INC.

New York   Toronto   London   Auckland   Sydney
Mexico City   New Delhi   Hong Kong   Buenos Aires

We put on our coats.
We are going out.

We are going on a hayride!

My brother says, "It is going to be spooky."

He says I will be scared.

It won't be spooky!
I won't be scared!

I hope.

My brother says there are
ghosts.
My brother says there are
monsters.

I say, "There is NO SUCH THING!"

My mom says we are
in a rush.
Time to go!

I see the **wagon**.
I see the **horses**.

I don't see ghosts.
I don't see monsters.

It's not spooky.

I find a place to sit.

My brother finds a place to sit.

The horses move.
The hayride starts.

The hayride goes
into the woods.

It is dark.
I hear a noise.
I see something white.

"What is that?"
"It's a ghost!"

It is only a sheet.

That's not spooky!

I see a campfire.
I see a shadow.
"What is that?"

"It's a monster!"

It is only a scarecrow!

That's not spooky!

We make a turn.
I can't see anything.

"What was that?"

It was me!
I am spooky!

Hayrides are fun!